7 STORIES

A PLAY BY
Morris Panych

Talonbooks   •   Vancouver   •   1990

Copyright © 1990 Morris Panych

Published with the assistance of the Canada Council of the Arts.

Talonbooks
P.O. Box 2076, Vancouver, British Columbia, Canada V6B 3S3
www.talonbooks.com

Typeset in Baskerville and printed and bound in Canada by
Hignell Book Printing.

Sixth Printing: August 2006

Canadian Cataloguing in Publication Data

Panych, Morris.
    Seven Stories

    A play.
    ISBN 0-88922-281-9

    I. Title.
PS8581.A65S4   1990   C812'.54   C90-091222-7
PR9199.3.P36S4 1990

ISBN-10: 0-88922-281-9
ISBN-13: 978-0-88922-281-6

7 STORIES

7 Stories was first produced at the Arts Club Theatre in Vancouver, B.C. in May, 1989 with the following cast:

Man	Peter Anderson
Charlotte Joan Nurse Wilson	Sherry Bie
Rodney Marshall Percy	David King
Jennifer Lillian Rachel	Wendy Gorling
Leonard Al Michael	Norman Browning

Directed by Morris Panych

Set Design by Ken MacDonald

Lighting Design by Marsha Sibthorpe

Costume Design by Nancy Tait

Original Music by Jeff Corness

Stage Manager: Marion Anderson

The action of the play takes place outside an apartment building — on the ledge, outside various windows of the seventh storey. As the play progresses, the lights emphasize the time elapsed between early evening and late night.

As the play opens, we hear a party in progress from one of the windows. MAN stands on the ledge, in a state of perplexity, contemplating the depths below. He seems disturbed, confused. Then he comes to what seems to be a resolution. He prepares to jump. As he is about to leap, the window next to him flies open. CHARLOTTE appears. She has a man's wallet, which she attempts to throw out the window. RODNEY, charging up from behind, grabs her hand. A window-ledge struggle ensues.

CHARLOTTE:
 Let GO of me!!! Let GO!!

RODNEY: *threatening*
 So-help-me-GOD-Charlotte . . . !!

CHARLOTTE: *daring him*
 What?? WHAT??!!

RODNEY:
 Give me back my wallet!

  She tries to throw it again. They struggle.

5

RODNEY:
What's WRONG with you? Are you CRAZY?!

CHARLOTTE:
YES! YES I AM!!!

RODNEY:
MY GOLD CARD is in there!!

CHARLOTTE:
Oh? Is it? Is your GOLD CARD in here . . .   *She searches through his wallet as he tries to retrieve it.*   Oh my goodness! So it is!! And your RACQUETCLUB membership!! Oooo! And a LOVELY picture of your LOVELY wife! We mustn't drop THAT, must we? We wouldn't want someone picking HER up off the street!!

RODNEY:
Give it here!

CHARLOTTE:
Leave me alone, or I'll call the police!

RODNEY:
You wouldn't dare.

CHARLOTTE:
HELP! POLICE!

RODNEY:
SHUT UP!!

CHARLOTTE:
You STRUCK me!!

RODNEY:
I did not!

CHARLOTTE:
Yes you did! He STRUCK me! HELP!

RODNEY:
> I did not!! SHUT UP!

CHARLOTTE:
> Yes you did! You bastard!

> *CHARLOTTE goes to strike him. They struggle violently out the window, as MAN watches on, in terror. RODNEY manages to grab CHARLOTTE by the throat and starts to strangle her.*

CHARLOTTE:
> HELP! Helgpjhhgghp!

RODNEY: *strangling her*
> You're quite unattractive when you're dying. Did you know that, Charlotte?

CHARLOTTE:
> Gddldjkiqk!!!

RODNEY: *calmly*
> You lose all your CHARM! You lose all your SPARKLE! Charlotte! I believe you're turning blue! It's most unbecoming!

CHARLOTTE:
> Gahhghh!

RODNEY:
> Is that all you've got to say, Charlotte? Ordinarily you're so outspoken. One might even say LOUD and CONSPICUOUS! What's that you say, Charlotte?

CHARLOTTE:
> Grrghaah!

RODNEY:
> Yes, the view from here is BREATH-TAKING, isn't it!

MAN:
> Excuse me.

RODNEY and CHARLOTTE are stopped cold.

MAN:
Would you mind letting go of her. You're hurting her.

RODNEY: *with feigned surprise*
Hurting her!?   *He looks at CHARLOTTE.*   Am I
hurting you, Charlotte?

CHARLOTTE:
Yeghhgg!

RODNEY: *letting go*
What's that Charlotte?

CHARLOTTE: *hoarsely*
Yes!

RODNEY:
I *am* sorry!   *to MAN*   You were right. I was hurting
her. And thank you for pointing that out. Why don't we go
inside, Charlotte? We seem to be attracting a crowd.

CHARLOTTE:
I am not going anywhere with you! You tried to KILL me!

RODNEY:
Kill you! Really Charlotte! Now why would I do that?
to MAN   She has an overactive imagination, you know.
Dabbles in the creative arts.

MAN:
Oh.

CHARLOTTE:
Dabbles!

RODNEY:
You're misinterpreting the facts once again, Charlotte.
to MAN   Apparently she misunderstood my intentions.
Come inside, Charlotte.

8

CHARLOTTE:
Misunderstood, nothing! You tried to kill me Rodney. He saw the whole thing. Didn't you?

MAN:
I —

CHARLOTTE:
He's a key witness. And we know all about key witnesses, don't we?   *to MAN*   Rodney's a lawyer.

MAN:
Oh.

RODNEY:
Charlotte! I'm warning you —

CHARLOTTE:
And of course we know all about lawyers, don't we?

MAN:
Actually, he's the only one I've ever met.

CHARLOTTE:
Really?!

RODNEY:
Oh, for heaven's sake!

CHARLOTTE:
Well, in that case, let me fill you in. Lawyers are the people who BORE you to death with the facts.   *to RODNEY*   By the way, Rodney. Why would you go to all the trouble of strangling me, when you simply could have BORED me to death?

RODNEY:
You're making a public spectacle!

CHARLOTTE:
My goodness that would have been the perfect crime. I would

have died, slowly, over the course of one of our romantic evenings together. Hanging, as it were, on his every word —

RODNEY:
I need a drink.

CHARLOTTE:
Would you like a drink?   *to Rodney*   Fix us a drink, would you Rodney?   *RODNEY goes*

MAN:
I —

CHARLOTTE:
Yes . . . I suppose you're wondering why I don't just leave him.

MAN:
Well, I —

CHARLOTTE:
That's a very good question.   *to RODNEY*   Rodney! What the gentleman wants to know is why I don't just leave you.

RODNEY:
Does he?

MAN:
I don't really —

CHARLOTTE:
Shall I tell him?

No answer.

CHARLOTTE:
He's not answering. He's standing there, giving me that LOOK again.   *to RODNEY*   Don't just stand there giving me that stupid LOOK. I'm not threatened by· you in the least.   *to MAN*   He thinks I'm threatened.
to RODNEY   In case you forgot, I have a key witness here who fully intends to testify at your attempted murder trial.

10

MAN:
I don't think I'll be around, I —

CHARLOTTE:
You won't? Why not?

RODNEY: *now at the window*
What a pity, Charlotte. Your KEY WITNESS won't be here.   *to MAN*   I can quite understand your reservations. Considering her history   *to CHARLOTTE* Get in here!!

CHARLOTTE:
Don't listen to him. He'll say anything. He spins a web of lies, like a spider.

RODNEY:
Really Charlotte. I'm surprised at your use of such a tired metaphor. And you call yourself a poet.

CHARLOTTE:
You see! He tries to make you lose your train of thought.

RODNEY:
I shouldn't think you'd need any help with that.

CHARLOTTE:
Where's my drink?

RODNEY:
Haven't you had enough.   *to MAN*   She loses count after ten cocktails.   *to CHARLOTTE*   Anyway, I'm leaving.

CHARLOTTE: *to MAN*
Ha!

RODNEY:
Where are my Italian brogues?

CHARLOTTE: *to MAN*
Most people wear shoes. *to RODNEY* I have no
idea. Perhaps I threw them out the window.

They all look down.

RODNEY:
Did you?

CHARLOTTE:
I honestly can't remember.

RODNEY:
You've hidden them. Where are they? *to MAN*
What's she done with my shoes?

MAN:
I —

CHARLOTTE:
I TOLD you — I can't remember. Besides — you happen to
be interrupting our conversation.

RODNEY:
Oh really? I'm sorry.

He goes.

MAN:
It's quite all right!

CHARLOTTE:
Don't pay any attention to him. As I was saying . . . the reason
I don't leave here is because Rodney and I are inseparable. The
question of leaving, although it arises constantly, is — dare I
say — moot. *to Rodney* MOOT? Is that right,
Rodney?

RODNEY:
WHAT!!?

CHARLOTTE:
Can I say "the question of my leaving is MOOT"?

RODNEY:
You can say whatever you like.

CHARLOTTE:
He's not usually so generous with my word usage. He finds himself correcting just about everything I say.

RODNEY: *correcting her*
Irrelevant!

CHARLOTTE:
What?

RODNEY:
The question of your leaving is irrelevant.

CHARLOTTE:
Thank you.   *to MAN*   You see.

MAN:
Yes, I see.

CHARLOTTE:
But I suppose you don't think the question is irrelevant? Since he just tried to kill me.

MAN:
Well —

CHARLOTTE:
Rodney!

RODNEY:
WHAT, for heaven's sake?!

CHARLOTTE:
He doesn't think the question of my leaving is irrelevant.

RODNEY:
Who doesn't?

CHARLOTTE:
He doesn't.

RODNEY:
Well, he doesn't know the facts.

CHARLOTTE:
Oh. Apparently you don't know the facts. Only Rodney, of
course, knows the facts. "The World According to Rodney."
My God. Where would we be without all those specific details?
Life would be so — vague. Perhaps even meaningless.

MAN:
Yes.

CHARLOTTE:
When you come to think of it, the Rodneys of this world are
man's salvation in a way. They build us the ramparts, stone by
stone, each one another absolute little certainty. Another "fact."
All piled high against the onslaught of the absurd truth!

RODNEY: *appearing with two drinks*
Really, Charlotte. You sound like a cheap novelist.

CHARLOTTE:
IT'S POETRY!!   *taking drinks*   Thank you.
Giving MAN one of the drinks.   Naturally he despises poetry.
He despises all art. Because art is the act of climbing to the top
of that ridiculous wall of his — and standing on the ledge —
to look out into a cruel and pointless world — devoid of meaning
— where fact is merely fiction. And anybody with any courage
would simply leap off the edge and be done with it.

RODNEY:
I could give you a little push if you'd like.

CHARLOTTE:
Go ahead and push me!

RODNEY goes.

MAN:
I wouldn't provoke him.

CHARLOTTE:
Oh good heavens. That would be much too quick for him. He'd rather kill me little by little than all at once.

RODNEY approaches from behind and points what seems to be a gun at the back of CHARLOTTE's head.

RODNEY:
One more word and I'll blow your head off.

CHARLOTTE:
I do hope that's a gun, Rodney, and not just your finger.

RODNEY:
That's our little secret. Now come inside. I don't want any witnesses this time.

CHARLOTTE:
Will you excuse us?

CHARLOTTE slowly closes the window. After a brief moment, a shot rings out.

As MAN stands, martini glass in hand, JENNIFER appears from the party window.

JENNIFER:
Was that gunfire?

MAN:
Uh — I don't . . .

JENNIFER: *looking down*
Was somebody gunned down, or what?

15

MAN:
> I'm not sure.

JENNIFER:
> I just LOVE your neighbourhood. It's so . . . third world!

LEONARD appears from his window, dressed in pyjamas.

LEONARD:
> SHUT UP!! SHUT UP for GOD'S SAKE!! SHUT UP!! I'm TRYING to get some SLEEP!!

JENNIFER:
> Oh, I know! I tried that once. Scary isn't it?

LEONARD:
> What's she talking about?

JENNIFER:
> I was just lying there . . . and I could hear myself breathing? You know? I thought Oh, God! I can hear myself breathing!! I'll never try THAT again!

LEONARD quietly closes his window.

JENNIFER:
> Wow! Your friend is so intense!

MAN:
> He's not —

JENNIFER: *looking down*
> Do you ever feel like throwing yourself out of a building?

MAN:
> *pause*

JENNIFER:
> Whenever I get too close to the edge, I just feel like jumping. Isn't that wild?!

MAN:

    pause

JENNIFER:

    It's probably symbolic.

MAN:

    pause

JENNIFER:

    Will you excuse me. It's not that I don't like you or anything
    — cause I really do — it's just that there's too many pauses in
    this conversation.

        She disappears, closing the window. After a moment, LEONARD
        opens his window.

LEONARD:

    Listen lady . . . where did she go? She wasn't even there. Oh,
    my God!   *to MAN*   She wasn't even there!

        He closes his window again. After a brief moment, he opens it again.

LEONARD:

    What do you want?

MAN:

    Uh . . .

LEONARD:

    A likely story! What?

MAN:

    I think there might have been a murder committed.

LEONARD:

    A murder! So THAT'S where she went.

MAN:

    No. Your neighbours.

LEONARD:
My neighbours murdered her!?

MAN:
No.

LEONARD:
She murdered my neighbours?

MAN:
It's got nothing to do with her. I think there's been a murder committed. I think you should call the police.

LEONARD:
Let me get this straight. You murdered the neighbours?

MAN:
I didn't say that!

LEONARD:
Yes, you did. Are you trying to tell me I'm hearing things? Is that what you're saying. I distinctly heard you say you murdered my neighbours. That it had nothing to do with her!

MAN:
All I said was: I think there's been a murder committed. There was an argument. Didn't you hear the gunshot?

LEONARD:
Gunshot! I didn't hear any gunshot! Are you sure it was a gunshot?

MAN:
Positive.

LEONARD:
Oh dear. This is a new twist. Usually I'm hearing things. Now, I'm *not* hearing things. Oh dear. I've gone deaf.

MAN:
Hadn't we better call the police?

LEONARD:
Did you say something just now?

MAN:
Yes.

LEONARD:
Are you sure?

MAN:
Of course I am. I said, we'd better call the police.

LEONARD:
Oh good. Well, I heard that quite distinctly. Every word of it.

MAN:
Look — this could be serious.

LEONARD:
Do you think so? I'm only a little tense. That's all. If I had some sleep I'd be just fine. Maybe it's just a little wax build-up.

MAN:
What are you talking about?

LEONARD:
What are *you* talking about? Aren't we both talking about the same thing?

MAN:
I was talking about your neighbours. About the gunshot.

LEONARD:
The gunshot! Yes! About whether I heard it or not.

MAN:
Look — that doesn't matter.

LEONARD:
It matters to me!

MAN:

There was a gunshot. That's all that matters. Just call the police!

LEONARD:

Now how can you expect me to do that? I didn't even hear a gunshot. What am I supposed to tell them   when and if they answer? Am I supposed to *admit* that I didn't even hear a gunshot from twenty feet away? Or am I supposed to pretend that I'm hearing things. They'll think I'm insane!

MAN:

What difference does it make?

LEONARD:

They ask for your name. Am I supposed to lie about that as well? They'll just find out anyway. Because they'll trace the call back to me. Why did I have to get dragged into this?

MAN:

Why are you taking it so personally? It's got nothing to do with you.

LEONARD:

Oh, that's right! Accuse me of being one of those!

MAN:

One of what?

LEONARD:

Those people who shut themselves off from the rest of the world.

MAN:

Good God! I wasn't accusing you of anything.

LEONARD:

Yes you were!

MAN:

No I wasn't!

LEONARD:

Are you positive about that?

MAN:

Of course I am. I don't even know you.

LEONARD:

There was a tone of accusation in your voice. You have to admit it.

MAN:

I think you're just being paranoid.

LEONARD:

Why would you say that?   *pause*   You don't know anything about paranoia. What experience do you have in that field — if any?

MAN:

None.

LEONARD:

A likely story!   *pause*   What did you say?

MAN:

I said I don't have any experience in the field.

LEONARD:

What's that supposed to mean?

MAN:

I mean I don't know anything about paranoia.

LEONARD:

Implying that I'm paranoid.

MAN:

Not at all.

LEONARD:
> By inference. Saying that you don't know anything about it. Inferring that I know a great deal.

MAN:
> You said so yourself.

LEONARD:
> I did not.

MAN:
> You indicated as much.

LEONARD:
> This is a trap! You're trying to trap me into something. Aren't you? You think I'm insane! That I've completely lost my grip on reality. And that's where you're wrong. I happen to be painfully cognizant of the world around me. I might be going deaf, but I'm not blind. I'm a qualified professional, and I'm trained to keep my eyes wide open.

> > *LEONARD instantly falls asleep. MAN studies LEONARD for a moment, then looking at his martini glass, goes back over to CHARLOTTE's window. He raps on the pane. RODNEY opens the window.*

RODNEY:
> What do YOU want?

MAN:
> Is everything all right?

RODNEY:
> Couldn't be better.

MAN:
> I heard a gunshot. I thought maybe there'd been an accident.

RODNEY:
> Charlotte!?

CHARLOTTE: *inside*
    What?!

RODNEY:
    The gentleman heard a gunshot. He thought there'd been an
    accident. Isn't that amusing?

CHARLOTTE:
    Ha! Ha!

RODNEY:
    As a matter of fact there was a bit of an accident. I aimed for
    her head and accidentally hit the wall. But thank you for your
    concern.

    RODNEY slams the window shut, waking LEONARD.

LEONARD:
    Ah! What happened?

MAN:
    I don't know. You fell asleep.

LEONARD:
    No I didn't. What?

MAN:
    You — fell — asleep.

LEONARD:
    I did? Well, of course I did! What did you expect?

MAN:
    I don't know.

LEONARD:
    That's right, you don't. I haven't slept more than two hours
    in the past month. I never sleep. I work nights.

MAN:
    So why don't you sleep during the day?

LEONARD:
Why do you want me to go to sleep?

MAN:
I don't. It makes no difference to me.

LEONARD:
Just what are you planning?

MAN:
Me? I'm not planning anything. I was only thinking . . . for your well-being . . .

LEONARD:
My well-being? You think I'm not well.

MAN:
I never said that.

LEONARD:
Somebody told you something, didn't they?

MAN:
No. Nobody told me anything.

LEONARD:
Why didn't they? Why would they want to keep YOU in the dark?

MAN:
Who?

LEONARD:
I don't know!! Has it occurred to you yet that you could be an innocent pawn in all this? A dupe?

MAN:
No.

LEONARD:
Well, you see! You're naive. You're the perfect candidate for them to carry out their insane plan.

MAN:

What insane plan?

LEONARD:

Well, they didn't tell you of course. They wouldn't want YOU to know!!

MAN:

Know what? Who's they?

LEONARD:

You said you heard a gunshot. Right?

MAN:

Yes. I did. But . . .

LEONARD:

Coming from where?

MAN:

Your neighbours, but . . .

LEONARD:

Well, they're in on it too. Don't you see?

MAN:

No. It's all been a mix-up. I mean, I heard a gunshot, but it turns out it was nothing.

LEONARD:

Nothing? You don't know what's going on in the world, do you?

MAN:

I used to think I did. I don't know. No . . . I don't.

LEONARD:

I suppose you think all these things happen by chance? Just one GREAT BIG HAPPY Coincidence. Gunshots are fired. Then they're not fired. A woman appears who was never there. That light in that apartment over there. I guess you didn't notice that either. Because you don't think these things are important.

MAN:
> Light?

LEONARD:
> Over there. It just went on. Don't look.

A slight pause as MAN considers this.

MAN:
> And?

LEONARD:
> And!? And WHAT?!

MAN:
> I don't get it.

LEONARD:
> Of course you don't get it. You don't know the code. Fortunately
> — I do. I have deciphered the code. I know EXACTLY what's
> going on. Ah. There goes that other light. Don't look.

MAN:
> There's lights going on and off all over the place. You don't think
> everybody's in on it.

LEONARD:
> In on WHAT? There IS something, isn't there?

MAN:
> I'm not really sure anymore.

LEONARD:
> And you think I'm confused!

MAN:
> I never said you were.

LEONARD:
> Well, who said I was, then?

MAN:

Nobody.

LEONARD:

Well, where did you get the information?

MAN:

I have no information. I don't know anything.

LEONARD:

Oh.   *pause*   Well, I don't know anything either. In fact, I don't even know what we were talking about.

MAN:

That makes two of us.

LEONARD:

Two of us?

MAN:

I don't know what you're talking about either.

LEONARD:

Oh.   *pause*   You don't?

MAN:

No.

LEONARD:

Was I being incoherent?

MAN:

I don't know what to say.

LEONARD:

What does that mean?

MAN:

You're bound to take it the wrong way.

LEONARD:
What?

MAN:
Whatever I say.

LEONARD:
What are you going to say?

MAN:
Nothing

LEONARD:
You can tell me. What is it? Is there something I should know about myself?

MAN:
Look — it's none of my business.

LEONARD:
What? What's none of your business?

MAN:
You asked if you were being incoherent. I don't know what to say. If I tell you, you were, you'll fly into a panic. If I tell you, you weren't, you'll think I'm trying to hide something from you. You take everything I say the wrong way.

LEONARD:
You think I'm insane.

MAN:
Now, there's a case in point. I don't think you're insane. I don't think anything. The word *insane* didn't even enter into it.

LEONARD:
Yes it did.

MAN:
Well, you said it. I didn't say it. I'm in no position to judge the state of your mind. I'm not a psychiatrist.

28

LEONARD:

A psychiatrist? Why did you mention a psychiatrist? I never said anything about a psychiatrist.

MAN:

I was only making a point.

LEONARD:

Well, you can make a point without mentioning a psychiatrist, can't you? You could have mentioned a proctologist.

MAN:

Why would I do that?

LEONARD:

Precisely!

MAN:

Very well, then. Have it your way. Let me correct myself. What I meant to say is: I'm in no position to judge the state of your mind. I'm not a proctologist. Is that better?

LEONARD:

Why are you making fun of me?

MAN:

I'm sorry.

LEONARD:

Do you find psychiatry amusing? Well, let me tell you — it's no joke.

MAN:

I didn't say it was.

LEONARD:

Oh, I realize, it's an easy target for satire. One might even say an obvious one. But it's serious work, involving a lot of time and dedication. And we don't get paid nearly as much as you'd like to think.

MAN:
You're a psychiatrist?

LEONARD:
Why do you say it like that? What are you implying?

MAN:
I'm not implying anything. I'm a little surprised. That's all.

LEONARD:
Why should you be? Do you think there's something strange
about it? Why are you looking at me like that?

MAN:
I'm not even looking at you.

LEONARD:
Why aren't you looking at me? Are you afraid of me? Are you
afraid I'll find something out about you? Some dark, terrible
secret? You can tell me — I'm a psychiatrist. Here — why don't
you take my card. You can set up an appointment with my
secretary. I work nights at the loony bin. But I have a private
practice in the mornings. I've got to run now. It's time to get
up and go to work. I haven't slept in three years but what
difference does that make to them? They're all on drugs. They
sleep all the time. I hate insane people. They drive me crazy.
I don't mean literally crazy. You didn't take that literally,
did you?

MAN:
No.

LEONARD:
Are you patronizing me?

MAN:
No.

LEONARD:
In the future, don't patronize me. I'm the doctor, and I'll do
all the patronizing. You'll find, once we've begun to develop

a professional relationship, that you'll come to rely on me for emotional support. I'll be carrying the weight of all your problems, so that you can feel free to let go. You won't have to hang onto your sanity. I'll be the one who's hanging on. That's my job.

LEONARD closes the window. The MAN studies the card. As he is pocketing the card, MARSHALL, wearing a tuxedo, opens another window and climbs out onto the ledge. Without noticing the MAN, he takes out a cigarette and lights it. For a moment he luxuriates in this obviously great pleasure. As he exhales he notices the MAN looking at him. MARSHALL speaks with a very "theatrical" accent.

MARSHALL:
Oh, pardon me. I hope you don't mind my smoking. It's my last cigarette.

MAN:
That's all right.

MARSHALL:
Would you like one?

MAN:
I don't know. I've never tried one before.

MARSHALL:
Here. Be my guest. You can take them all.

MAN: *making his way a little along the ledge*
I guess it can't do any harm now.

MARSHALL:
And *I* certainly won't be smoking them.   *He hands the MAN his cigarettes.*

Suddenly, LEONARD's window opens once again, behind him.

31

LEONARD:
> I have a question I forgot to ask you.   *Not noticing that he has moved.*   My God! He wasn't even there!

MAN:
> I'm over here. I'm having a cigarette.

LEONARD:
> Who's that?

MAN:
> A gentleman. I don't know his name. We only just met.

MARSHALL:
> It's Marshall. Actually, it's Mike.

LEONARD:
> Well, who is he?

MAN:
> I don't know. We only just met.   *Now he climbs along the ledge, a little way back to LEONARD's window.*   What was your question?

LEONARD:
> What question?

MAN:
> You have a question you forgot to ask me.

LEONARD:
> What sort of question?

MAN:
> I don't know.

LEONARD:
> Well, what? Was it a personal question?

MAN:
> *You* were the one who wanted to ask it.

LEONARD:

Then it *was* personal

MAN:

I really don't know.

LEONARD:

Could I have a word with you for a moment.

MAN:

What is it?

LEONARD: *sotto voce*

What does he want?

MAN:

I don't think he wants anything. I think he's just having a cigarette.

LEONARD:

Does he know about our conversation?

MAN:

No. I don't think so.

LEONARD:

Well, don't say a word to him. Keep it private.

MAN:

All right.

LEONARD:

We must pretend that we never spoke.

MAN:

We're speaking now.

LEONARD:

Act like you don't know me.

MAN:
> I don't.

LEONARD:
> Otherwise, he might get the wrong idea. He'll think that just because, you're seeing a psychiatrist that you're insane. And that kind of information can get into the wrong hands.

> *Without saying another word, LEONARD slowly closes the window, putting his finger to his lips in a secret gesture.*

MARSHALL: *who has been watching*
> Friend of yours?

MAN:
> No. I don't know him.

MARSHALL:
> Best to keep it that way. People know far too much about each other these days. I much prefer to form my own false impressions. Don't you?

MAN:
> I really don't like to speculate.

MARSHALL:
> What difference does it make? The truth is irrelevant. One's own opinion on the other hand is far more appealing. One should always form a strong opinion, one way or the other. Regardless of the facts.

MAN:
> That seems to be a popular theme around here.

MARSHALL:
> After all, it's about the only thing people are entitled to. Except for me. I've completely relinquished my personality. I've even relinquished my hair colour. Can you believe it?

MAN:
> That's not your real hair colour?

MARSHALL:

Oh, there's no need to pretend you didn't know.

MAN:

I didn't.

MARSHALL:

I won't be offended if you don't like it. I'm not that sort of person. But you can decide what sort of person I am for yourself. And anyway — it's got nothing to do with me. It's my wife's decision really. Well, it's not really a decision. But then, she's not really my wife, is she? Not yet. But almost.

MAN:

You're getting married.

MARSHALL:

Yes. In a little over half an hour, my life, as you and I know it, will be over. Finished. Butted out. Extinguished.

MAN:

I suppose congratulations are in order.

MARSHALL:

Don't be absurd. Congratulations aren't in order at all. On the other hand, I don't expect any sympathy. You wouldn't feel the least bit sorry for me if you knew the whole story.   *Suddenly switching to another, more natural voice.*   Is my moustache on straight?

MAN:

It looks fine.

MARSHALL: *returning to accent*

Of course it doesn't look fine. Don't be ridiculous. I'm only asking if it's straight. This damn glue doesn't stick properly.

MAN:

You mean it's false?

MARSHALL:
Couldn't you tell?   *normal voice*

MAN:
No.

MARSHALL: *accent*
Oh good. Of course, I suppose it'll fall off in the middle of the ceremony, and that'll be the end of it. I really ought to have grown one. But I can't stand moustaches. The itching drives me mad. Oh God. I've only got half a cigarette left! It seems to be burning awfully fast. Isn't that always the way? You're not smoking yours.

MAN:
I'm sorry. I don't find it very pleasant.

MARSHALL: *normal voice*
Well, don't waste it, for God's sake. Here. I'll finish it.

MARSHALL now has two cigarettes, which he smokes alternately.

MARSHALL: *as he continues to speak he gradually loses his accent*
If I had the time, I'd smoke the whole pack. But the Best Man is waiting for me. He thinks I'm in the bathroom. Thank God for bathrooms. Where would we be without them, eh? Those little private oases in the desert of eternal wedlock. Wedlock! There's a good name for it. Sounds like padlock, doesn't it? What a perfect description for marriage. Wed — *Lock*. The penitentiary of betrothal! I imagine I'll be spending the rest of my life locked in a bathroom somewhere. Oh, there's no need to be concerned about it. The house has seven different bathrooms. Excluding the *en suites*.

MAN:
No. It's not that.

MARSHALL:
What is it, then? You look troubled.

MAN:

I'm sorry. It's no business of mine, but why are you wearing a false moustache?

MARSHALL:

Well, it's part of my character, isn't it?

MAN:

It is?

MARSHALL:

He wears a moustache. His hair is auburn. And he doesn't smoke, among other things. And his name is Marshall. And I keep losing my accent.

MAN:

You mean to say that's not your real accent?

MARSHALL: *accent*

Well, it is now. Now that I've fully adopted this character.

MAN:

You had *me* fooled.

MARSHALL:

That's the idea

MAN:

It's so realistic.

MARSHALL: *changes to normal voice*

Well, there's a lot at stake, isn't there?

MAN:

There is?

MARSHALL:

About a hundred and fifty million, I'd say. Give or take a million. But who's counting?

MAN:
Dollars?

MARSHALL:
Dollars. Debentures. Stocks. Bonds. Futures. Securities. You name it.

MAN:
Yours?

MARSHALL:
If I play my part well enough. If the moustache doesn't fall off at the altar.

MAN:
And what if it does?

MARSHALL:
Then they'll wonder, won't they? Wouldn't you?

MAN:
Well, yes. I'm wondering now.

CHARLOTTE bursts forth.

CHARLOTTE:
Help!

MARSHALL: *assuming accent again*
Are you in some sort of trouble, madam?

CHARLOTTE:
Help me.

MARSHALL:
Should I call the police this time?

CHARLOTTE:
He tried to kill me!

MARSHALL:
>Oh, dear. Again?

MAN:
>Again?

>*Off-stage, we hear a little girl's voice.*

EFFIE:
>Marshall!! Marshall!!

MARSHALL: *Own voice. To MAN.*
>It's that horrible little flower girl. Will you excuse me.
>*He goes.*

MAN:
>Again?

CHARLOTTE:
>What?

MAN:
>You mean to say he's tried to kill you before.

CHARLOTTE:
>On several occasions. Not the least of which was my
>BIRTHDAY!!

RODNEY: *from off*
>Oh, for heaven's sake . . . get in here!!

CHARLOTTE:
>Don't you think that's insensitive?

MAN:
>Well, yes, I . . .

CHARLOTTE:
>Rodney!

RODNEY:
What!?

CHARLOTTE:
This gentlemen thinks it's incredibly insensitive that you tried to kill me on my birthday.

RODNEY:
Oh, does he?

MAN:
I —

RODNEY:
He doesn't know the whole story.

CHARLOTTE:
Oh. You don't know the whole story.

RODNEY:
And what's more, it wasn't your birthday.

CHARLOTTE:
It was MY BIRTHDAY!! He has a tremendous sense of occasion.

RODNEY:
You're distorting the facts once again.

MAN:
Why do you treat each other this way?

CHARLOTTE:
It's all words and gestures. Pomp. There's absolutely no substance to it.

MAN:
He was choking you to death.

CHARLOTTE:
Oh, that. It gives him a tremendous sense of power to hear me gasping helplessly for air.

MAN:
   And the gun?

CHARLOTTE:
   Blanks.

MAN:
   You were both just pretending?

CHARLOTTE:
   Oh, I don't know. There's such a fine line between truth and
   fiction, isn't there. It's the subject of a number of foreign
   films.   *to RODNEY*   Oh, for God's sake, Rodney.
   What are you doing now?

RODNEY:
   I'm killing all your goldfish.

CHARLOTTE:
   Did you hear that? He's killing all my goldfish.

MAN:
   Yes. I heard.

CHARLOTTE:
   The neighbours can hear you, Rodney.

RODNEY:
   What? Killing a fish?

CHARLOTTE:
   He's not really doing anything. He's standing there *looking* at
   my goldfish. Giving them that LOOK. That DEADLY LOOK.
   Yes. I was only acting.

MAN:
   Pardon?

CHARLOTTE:
   I was pretending to die. He finds it amusing.

MAN:
   Oh. Well, I don't.

CHARLOTTE:
   Then why were you watching us?

MAN:
   I happened to be here. That's all.

CHARLOTTE:
   I see.

RODNEY: *inside*
   Come inside, Charlotte. I've got a knife and I want to cut your
   head off.

CHARLOTTE: *to RODNEY*
   That knife isn't even sharp. You'd have to poke my head off
   with that!

RODNEY:
   Now there's an idea!

CHARLOTTE:
   He's threatening to cut my head off with a butter knife. Can
   you imagine?!

MAN:
   No, not really.

CHARLOTTE:
   Well, at least it's something. I suppose there's a certain affection
   in it. It keeps the relationship alive anyway. It used to be one
   of those dreary, mindless little affairs that start with a bang, and
   end with a whimper. We weren't even lovers anymore. Just
   zombies. You can't imagine. He started reading the paper at
   dinner. I started having another affair. You can't believe how
   complicated that is. Cheating on the man you're cheating with.
   Anyway — it had all the trappings of a marriage. Which is
   precisely what both of us were trying to escape. We began to
   dread seeing one another. Finally, I suppose out of sheer

exasperation, dear Rodney, the boring lawyer, tried to run me down with his car. It's hard to explain, but as I lay on the curb, half-conscious, I felt — revitalized. We both did. And we've been trying to kill each other ever since.

RODNEY:
Charlotte . . . ?

CHARLOTTE: *to MAN*
It's not entirely an act. We really do hate each other. But there's something to be said for that, isn't there. There's a certain zeal to it.

CHARLOTTE leaves.

MARSHALL returns, now speaking in his normal voice.

MARSHALL:
They're quite an item, those two.

MAN:
You know them?

MARSHALL:
I've seen them around. She tried to stab him to death in the hallway last week. It's really an incredible love story.

MAN:
Love?

MARSHALL:
What would you call it?

MAN:
I —

MARSHALL:
Oh. I forgot. You don't like to speculate on these things.

MAN:
No.

43

MARSHALL:

I do. I think they're deeply and passionately in love, and I think that one day soon, quite by accident, there will be casualties. It's not my kind of love, mind you. I'm much more inclined toward the romantic. The sentimental. The sort of love that brings a tear to the eye. Like a good television commercial. Counterfeit emotion is really my style. Counterfeit everything.

MAN:

Like your moustache?

MARSHALL:

It is perfect when you think about it.

MAN:

What is?

MARSHALL:

This masquerade.

MAN:

Wouldn't it be easier just to be who you are?

MARSHALL:

I wonder what that would be? Anyway — it wouldn't be what she wants. This is what she wants so this is what she gets. After all, I'm being well compensated for it. So what do I care? It's no worse than what I was doing. Just a little more involved.

MAN:

What were you doing?

MARSHALL:

Acting. I was acting for a living.

MAN:

Oh. You're an actor.

MARSHALL:

Well, not anymore. I've forfeited that as well. Along with my

name. It used to be Mike. Michael Merchant. I take it you've
never heard of me.

MAN:

I, uh . . . . .

MARSHALL:

But then, why would you have? I was never really very good.
Quite second-rate, in fact. I've played all the great roles, but
I've played them all very badly. Acting is such a desperately futile
profession anyway. Playing out the lives of other men. Knowing
of their failures and successes long before they ever do. Living,
suffering, murdering, dying . . . all in the space of three hours.
Sometimes only two. And in such a confined little area. And
over and over again every night. Can you imagine anything more
perfectly stupid? Squeezing a whole existence into a measly
evening's entertainment on the stage? And not only that — in
the middle of it all — pausing for an intermission. It makes one's
own life seem unbearably preposterous, doesn't it?

MAN:

Yes. I suppose it does.

MARSHALL:

So I'm more than happy to give it up.

MAN:

But you're acting now.

MARSHALL:

Well, yes, but this is different, isn't it?

MAN:

Is it?

MARSHALL:

Most certainly and definitely. This is one play where the curtain
never goes down. I will play this character until I die. Or until
she does. But that's another story.

JOAN and MICHAEL burst forth from another window, struggling with an antique vase.

JOAN:
No. No, Michael. Please!

MICHAEL:
Pull yourself together, Joan. Be a little more objective.

JOAN:
Michael . . . Michael . . .

MICHAEL:
Joan!

In their struggle, the vase breaks.

JOAN:
Oh, no. It was family!

MICHAEL:
Yes, but it was completely out of fashion.

JOAN:
It meant a great deal to me, Michael.

MICHAEL:
My mother meant a great deal to me, Joan, but she didn't go with anything either.

They go.

MAN:
I don't get it. I just can't understand why your fiancée would want you to be someone else.

MARSHALL:
She doesn't want me to be someone else. As far as she's concerned, I *am* someone else. I'm Marshall. She doesn't know anything about Michael Merchant, and she never will. In about

46

five minutes from now, Michael Merchant will disappear from the face of the earth. He'll be nothing but a fleeting memory.

MAN:
Where will he go?

MARSHALL:
That's probably a very interesting philosophical question. But I'm not a philosopher. I'm Marshall.

MAN:
So you said.

MARSHALL:
Yes. Well, it doesn't hurt to remind myself. *normal voice* She first met me, that is, she first met *him* one night about a year ago. I was playing Horatio, and as usual, playing it very badly. Not only that — but on this particular evening, I was also playing it very fast. The flights of angels had never so quickly sung poor Hamlet to his rest. I had a date with destiny, you see. Actually, I had a date with a sailor.

MAN:
A sailor? A *male* sailor?

MARSHALL:
Yes. It's funny, now that I think about it. Well, it's all an act anyway. Isn't it? The whole stupid dumb show. Life, I mean. His name was Marshall. And it was him I was thinking about, as I dashed from the theatre, still in make-up and in this ridiculous hair colour, and moustache, when this sleek, red Mercedes came roaring around the corner . . .

MAN:
So she hit you.

MARSHALL:
Almost hit me. But she'll never know. I must say — it was a much better performance than the one I'd just given. And I thought — well, a Mercedes . . . there's got to be a little money here somewhere. And as it turns out, there was. Quite a little.

47

MAN:
A hundred and fifty million.

MARSHALL:
It does come trippingly off the tongue, doesn't it? Like the name Marshall. It seemed to suit the scenario. More like the name of the sort of person who might be worth her while. Anyway, it worked. She loved the name, she loved the hair colour, and she adored the moustache. And the rest of the character just slowly fell into place, until it was exactly what she wanted. She couldn't have done better if she'd ordered me from a catalogue, which is just the sort of thing she usually does. Who'd believe it, eh?

MAN:
I would think she's bound to find out the truth.

MARSHALL:
Well, as I say. Who'd believe it?

MAN:
But what about family and friends?

MARSHALL:
They go with the forfeit. Vanish into thin air.

MAN:
They'll see you in the street.

MARSHALL:
We'll hardly be travelling in the same circles. And if they ever do see me, I'll simply remind them of someone they used to know.

MAN:
But what about records of birth. That sort of thing. Don't you have to prove who you are? Even to get a marriage license?

MARSHALL:
I have a friend in props. He's very good.

MAN:

Well, you can't just appear out of nowhere. What about parents?

MARSHALL:

Yes. Those were difficult parts to cast.

MAN:

You mean, there are others in on this?

MARSHALL:

Oh, just a couple of old actors, in need of a steady job. I have to admit *she's* a bit of a ham. Calls me "son" too much. But I've passed it off as eccentricity. The inlaws find them terribly charming. And there's an uncle. He's an old friend of mine. I owe him a few favours, so he's part of the family now. It's quite a collection. Between them, they've come up with more than a few fond memories of my childhood.

MAN:

This is total fraud!

MARSHALL:

Well, we're looking at it more like a long run.

MAN:

What's more, it's immoral!

MARSHALL:

Don't be ridiculous. It's nothing of the kind. It's simply patronage of the arts. It all depends on your point of view. And anyway, no one's doing anyone any harm.

MAN:

But you've given up your family. Your friends. You're making a complete mockery out of your existence. A joke. Doesn't your life mean anything?

MARSHALL:

Well, I've lived so many, haven't I? Lives are just short little episodes. You're on and then you're off. Just like that. Which reminds me. I'm off.

Just as MARSHALL is leaving, RACHEL opens her window.

RACHEL:
Oh, excuse me.

LEONARD reappears as RACHEL closes her window.

LEONARD:
Oh good. You're still here.   *producing pills*   Here take
a couple of these.

MAN:
What are they?

LEONARD:
Oh, you know. The usual.

MAN:
There's nothing wrong with me. Nothing — psychiatric. I don't
really have any of the necessary symptoms.

LEONARD: *another bottle*
Then you'll want to take a couple of these first before you take
a couple of those. Otherwise, there's no reason to take any of
those. These ones pick you up and those ones bring you down.
So it's really better if you take them both at the same time. That'll
keep you more or less balanced until I get back from the booby
hatch.

He goes. MAN studies the pills. RACHEL opens her window.

RACHEL:
How long are you going to be out there? Roughly speaking?

MAN:
Huh?

RACHEL:
Are you going to be out there for long?

50

MAN:
    I have no idea.

RACHEL:
    Oh. Well, don't rush. I can wait.

    Pause.

RACHEL:
    Will it be more than ten minutes?

MAN:
    What?

RACHEL:
    Will it be more than ten minutes, or less than ten minutes?

MAN:
    I don't really know.

RACHEL:
    Oh.

    A pause. She watches, as he contemplates the depths.

RACHEL:
    So you really don't know how long you'll be.

MAN:
    Does it make any difference?

RACHEL:
    No. I suppose not. Not if you're preoccupied.

MAN:
    Preoccupied?

RACHEL:
    With your thoughts.

MAN:
Oh. Yes. I am.

RACHEL:
You have your thoughts and you need somewhere to think them.
Someplace private, I understand,

MAN:
You do?

RACHEL:
Well, of course. I value my privacy, too. A person needs to be
alone with God.

MAN:
God.

RACHEL:
So go ahead. I'm not going to bother you anymore.

As he contemplates, she lowers money on a string.

MAN: *muttering to himself*
Monday, Tuesday, Thursday, Friday . . .   *Noticing the*
money.   What are you doing?

RACHEL: *retrieving money*
Oh. it's nothing. Really.

MAN:
What *is* that?

RACHEL:
What?

MAN:
In your hand?

RACHEL:
Are you asking me what I've got in my hand? Is that what you
want to know?

MAN:

Yes. Well, no. Well, I know what you've got. You've got some money.

RACHEL:

Well, then you don't need to ask.

MAN:

On a string?

RACHEL:

I thought you had some thinking to do?

MAN:

I do. But I just couldn't help noticing. That's all.

RACHEL:

I'm sorry if I was distracting you.

MAN:

Well, it's not my place, really. I mean — I don't belong here. It's your business what you do with your money. If you want to lower it on a string that's your business.

RACHEL:

It does seem odd from this perspective, I'll admit; when you see it from above. You're getting the seventh-storey perspective. If you were on the sixth storey, this would look quite different.

MAN:

Yes. I'm sure it would.

RACHEL:

But please don't let me interrupt. You were in the middle of prayer.

MAN:

No, I wasn't. If fact I'm not even sure I believe in God.

RACHEL:

Sometimes in a person's life, they're not really sure. They lose their faith. They become pragmatic about things. They need hard evidence of God's existence. But the evidence of God is everywhere.

MAN:

Where?

RACHEL:

Well, since you asked about the money, I'll tell you. There's a man here. Just below us. On the sixth floor? Last night, he turned to God for help. He's in a great deal of trouble. He drinks quite heavily, you see. His wife left him three years ago. Then he lost his job. He was a carpet wholesaler, or a carp-fish processor. I'm not really sure. He slurs his words quite a bit. Last year his son was killed on a motorbike. Or murdered with a knife. And six months ago, a close friend of his, was killed in what sounds like a freak accident, involving either a stray piece of glass, or the spraying of some gas, or a suspension bridge collapse. And now, they're evicting him. He's asked for money. And God is answering. Could the evidence be clearer?

MAN:

It's not clear to me.

RACHEL:

Unfortunately, you're on the wrong floor. I can't help people up here on the seventh storey. But the people on the sixth and fifth are well looked-after.

MAN:

You're answering all their prayers?

RACHEL:

Not all. I try to spread things around a little. A toaster here, an electric heater there. Besides, they can't have everything they ask for. I've only got so much. And I wouldn't want them taking it for granted. Miracles don't just happen, you know. They require a great deal of prayer. Even little miracles.

MAN:

But you can't expect people to believe that this is God's work.

They might as well believe in Santa Claus! And what's the procedure if they don't believe? Do you lower down over-due electric bills and eviction notices?

A pause.

MAN:
You didn't!

RACHEL:
What difference does it make?

MAN:
You sent him that eviction notice?

RACHEL:
I'm giving him the rent money. Everything will be fine now. He was lost and now he's found.

MAN:
Lost! The poor man lost his wife, his job, his son, his best friend. Isn't that punishment enough? You weren't involved with any of that, were you?

RACHEL:
That's so typical.

MAN:
What is?

RACHEL:
It's just so easy to be cynical, isn't it?

MAN:
Under the circumstances.

RACHEL:
These people's lives have changed! You've never heard so many prayers as the ones that rise up from directly below this window.

MAN:
No. I don't doubt it.

RACHEL:
And that is the power of faith!

MAN:
What is? Hoping for a toaster? How do you know it isn't the power of greed?

RACHEL:
I don't know who you are, and I don't know who sent you, but I have a pretty good idea. And you're not going to alter my relationship with God.

MAN:
I have no interest in your relationship with God.

RACHEL:
You want to make me say something, but I won't.

MAN:
I don't want to make you say anything. Don't be ridiculous. What on earth would I want you to say?

RACHEL:
Oh, you know perfectly well.

MAN:
No I don't

RACHEL:
Yes you do.

PERCY appears, from party window.

PERCY:
Say — where did you get that drink? I've been looking everywhere. Nobody's drinking anything. Is this a new trend or what? First nobody was smoking, so I had to give up smoking. I never really liked smoking, you know, but everybody was smoking, so I

started smoking, and then I got hooked. Then everybody was quitting so I had to quit. And now it looks like nobody's drinking. Everybody's walking. Everybody used to run. I'm glad that's over. Now everybody is walking. Nobody's running anymore. Well, I guess because everybody's getting older. Well — nobody's getting younger, that's for sure! Yeah — everybody's in the same boat, and nobody's rocking it anymore. Everybody used to rock the boat. Everybody used to be different from everybody else, so nobody would be the same. But that didn't work, because everybody was the same, because everybody was different. Now everybody is just plain "the same." Except for you. You're drinking. I wish I was.

RACHEL:
You've got your priorities all wrong, mister. You don't need a drink. You need God.

PERCY:
God? Nobody's doing God! Okay — *some* people were doing God, but not everybody. And that was before everybody was doing sex and hardly anybody's doing sex anymore. Everybody's doing children. Children — and walking — and gas ranges. Not God!

He goes.

RACHEL:
He's the devil.

MAN:
No he's not.

RACHEL:
Well, he's not actually the devil. The devil doesn't make personal appearances. He acts through people.

MAN:
What? You don't think that people are capable of acting on their own? You think the devil sent me?

RACHEL:
Can you think of any other explanation?

MAN:
Yes. I can.

RACHEL:
Well, of course you can. You could probably come up with at least a dozen reasons why you're standing on the ledge outside my window. He's very good at making even the most perverse things seem perfectly reasonable.

MAN:
Well, if you must now the truth . . .

RACHEL:
The truth! How clever! Go ahead. Try and seduce me.

MAN:
Seduce you. I haven't got the slightest interest in you.

RACHEL:
You know what I mean.

MAN:
No. I don't.

RACHEL:
Try and convince me that God doesn't exist.

MAN:
Why would I do that? No. Really. Why would I try and convince you that God doesn't exist? In the first place, I don't care whether you believe in him or not. In the second place, I'm not really sure myself.

RACHEL:
This is amazing! You are so devious. Pretending that you don't care. Even pretending that you sort of believe in God yourself.

MAN:
But I'm not pretending.

RACHEL:

And even pretending that you're *not* pretending.

MAN:

This is hopeless.

RACHEL:

Yes. It's hopeless. You won't make me say it.

MAN:

Say *what?*

RACHEL:

Well, I'm not going to say it, am I?

MAN:

How do I know if I don't even know what you're going to say?

RACHEL:

I have to admit that you're very shrewd. You think that if you act stupid enough, that somehow I'll confess to my doubts. But you'll never make me.

MAN:

If I'm not mistaken, you already have.

RACHEL:

I have not.

MAN:

You said that you'll confess to your doubts.

RACHEL:

You've turned this whole thing inside out.

MAN:

Well, I won't argue the point. I really don't care. I was merely concerned about the effects of your faith on other people. Especially poor, desperate people.

RACHEL:
What do you know about desperate people? When have you ever
been desperate? Ask *me* about desperation. I'll tell you all about
it. God has tested my faith in many horrible ways! He has sent
me almost every disease imaginable. He has crippled me, and
bruised me, and pushed me around. And, as if that isn't enough,
he shoved my mother down a flight of stairs, and turned her into
a human vegetable. I had to care for her. I had to change her
dirty clothes and feed her like a baby. She was my daily torment
for sixteen years, until finally, out of sheer divine mercy, he gave
her an overdose of two thousand milligrams of diazepam!

> *RACHEL cries. THE MAN is in shock at what RACHEL has
> just told him. Another window opens. JOAN, holding two bolts
> of cloth, leans out the window.*

JOAN:
It's even worse in the street light, darling. There's *red* in it!

MICHAEL: *from inside*
Oh, please! Are you blind?

JOAN:
It's not beige at all. It's pink! Look!

MICHAEL: *appearing*
Why do I even argue with you? It's pointless!

JOAN:
But can't you see the red?

MICHAEL:
It's the reflection of the neon, dear. There's too much bounce
out here from the lights. Where's your sense of colour?

JOAN:
Well, what's wrong with this other shade?

MICHAEL:
It's not a *shade*! It's a tint for heaven's sake! Please!

JOAN:
What's wrong with it?

RACHEL cries.

MAN: *to RACHEL*
Stop crying for heaven's sake!

MICHAEL and JOAN stop, and notice the MAN, who smiles back.

JOAN:
Are we interrupting something?

MAN:
No. Nothing. Sorry. Carry on.

RACHEL:
No one will ever destroy my faith! Not you — not even God!

JOAN:
At least let her have her faith, for heaven's sake.

MAN:
She can have it. I'm not stopping her.

JOAN:
What sort of faith are we talking about anyway?

RACHEL:
My faith in God.

JOAN:
Oh. How interesting. Well, I know what it's like.

MICHAEL:
Yes. She has absolutely no faith in me!

JOAN:
Don't be ridiculous, Michael. Of course I do!

MICHAEL:

Then why don't you believe me when I tell you this has absolutely no pink tones?!

JOAN:

Because it does! *To RACHEL and the MAN* Would you mind giving us your opinion?

MICHAEL: *insulted*

Really Joan! You're not serious. You can't be!

JOAN:

I'm only asking.

MICHAEL: *about to cry throughout, head, hand*

This is an outrage!

drama queen

He leaves the window.

JOAN:

Oh dear. I've upset him. Excuse me.   *she leaves*
Michael!

MAN:

That's murder, you know.

RACHEL:

What is?!

MAN:

Giving your mother an overdose of diazepam. That's cold-blooded murder.

RACHEL:

I didn't give her an overdose. *She* took the pills.

MAN:

Oh!

RACHEL:

She wanted to die, so God gave her the strength to do it.

62

MAN:

Suicide is not an act of God.

RACHEL:

How do you know?

MAN:

Because it's a human act. It's the one act that defies all predestiny. And it's got nothing to do with anybody else. It stands alone. Complete and of itself. What are you doing?

RACHEL:

I'm praying.

MAN:

Well, please don't. You're wasting your time. Unless there's somebody just like you up on the eighth floor. Look. Please. Don't bother.

RACHEL:

Do you want to go to Hell someday?

MICHAEL returns, leaning out of the window, sulking.

JOAN: *from behind*

Michael. Please. I'm sorry.

RACHEL:

Well, I can't help you if you want to go to Hell.

JOAN:

I'm sorry darling.

MICHAEL:

Go ahead and make a fool out of me. See if I care.

JOAN:

Nobody's trying to make a fool out of you.

MICHAEL: *referring to the MAN*

What does *he* know about hue? About value, or intensity? About

63

pair interpretation, for that matter? It's all subjective with him. Low and common. Is that what you want? The lowest common denominator? Consensus? A thousand people all shouting "beige! beige!"? And who asks the all-important question "which beige?"? Someone's got to ask that question, Joan. Or the world becomes nothing. Just a ugly great wash!

RACHEL: *to MAN*
If you change your mind and decide to go to Heaven, let me know.

> *RACHEL closes her window.*

MICHAEL:
Heaven? My goodness — she has a very high opinion of herself.

MAN:
She was speaking theologically.

JOAN: *to MICHAEL*
Am I forgiven, then?

MICHAEL:
You must stop questioning my stylistic perceptions.

JOAN:
I don't.

MICHAEL:
You can't just go out and buy an ashtray — or a vase.

JOAN:
I can't help it.

MICHAEL:
You've got to learn to disassociate yourself with your emotions a little and finally come to terms with style.

JOAN:
I'm trying, Michael. I'm really trying.

MICHAEL:

And you can't just go asking any idiot off the street what he thinks.

JOAN:

Well, he looked like he might be objective.

MICHAEL:

But what does he know about the physiological capacities? What does he know about black, about white? About anything at all, for that matter? He's nothing but an animal, in an animal world.

They both study the MAN.

MICHAEL:

Look at the way he's dressed. Can you seriously take his word for anything?

MAN:

What's wrong with the way I'm dressed?

JOAN:

Nothing darling. You look perfectly charming.

MICHAEL:

There's no thought. There's no justification. It's all mood. Stream of consciousness.

MAN:

I beg your pardon . . .

MICHAEL:

He's a walking fatality. A casualty of function!

MAN:

Excuse me . . .

JOAN:

Yes?

MAN:

Well, I couldn't help overhearing you.

MICHAEL:

I'm sorry. I was just being emphatic.

JOAN:

Michael is very emphatic.

MAN:

If I'm not mistaken, you called me an idiot.

JOAN:

Try not to take it personally, darling.

MICHAEL:

I wasn't referring to you. You're no more idiotic than the next person.

MAN:

I don't mind being called an idiot. It's not that. It's just that you don't know me.

MICHAEL:

Well, no. I don't. Why on earth would I?

MAN:

Well, if you don't know me, how do you know I'm an idiot? What if I said you were an idiot?

MICHAEL:

You'd be an idiot for saying it.   *back to JOAN*   Now, let's discuss this green thing for a moment. I'm not entirely adverse, but you must remember that unlike nature, where it's so pervasively vital, green can take on a role of defensiveness and obstinacy. It has it's devious side.

JOAN:

But don't you think it reflects my character?

MICHAEL:

The character of a colour depends entirely on the colours around it. You can't take a colour out of context.

MAN:

Just how is it that you can call me an idiot, but if I call you an idiot, then I'm an idiot for saying it?

MICHAEL: *to MAN*

Do you mind?   *to JOAN*   Who *is* this man?

JOAN:

I suppose he's a neighbour. Are you a neighbour?

MAN:

No. And there's nothing wrong with the way I'm dressed, either.

MICHAEL:

Nobody said there was. I don't make value judgements. I'm not a fascist.

JOAN:

Michael never makes value judgements.

MAN:

I didn't say you were a fascist.

JOAN:

He's just being sensitive, aren't you Michael?

MICHAEL:

I'm not *being* sensitive. I *am* sensitive.

JOAN:

Of course you are.

MAN:

I merely took exception to your sweeping generalizations. About me — and about the world at large. After all — you said I was nothing but an animal, in an animal world.

MICHAEL: *angry*
     I can't deal with this Joan.

JOAN:
     Of course you can't. You go inside for a moment, darling, while
     I send the gentleman away.

          MICHAEL goes.

MICHAEL: *hold back tears*
     I just can't deal with it.

MAN:
     What's he so upset about? I'm the one who's been insulted.

JOAN:
     Of course you have. Can I write you a cheque or do you want
     cash?

MAN:
     Why would I want cash?

JOAN:
     Good. I'll write you a cheque, then.

MAN:
     I don't want a cheque either.

JOAN:
     No? Well, what do you want?

MAN:
     Nothing.

JOAN:
     Oh. How interesting.

MAN:
     I certainly don't want money.

JOAN:

I'm sorry if my offer offended you. It's just that . . . so often, in situations involving Michael, it's much more expedient to simply buy one's way out.

MAN:

Does he always go around insulting people?

JOAN:

Michael is an artist. People don't understand him. He's intensely visual. The sight of red with yellow gives him heart palpitations. Certain shades of magenta make him physically nauseous. He can feel the space around him so much so that he becomes the space. The presence of Dacron gives him the flu. So you can imagine how difficult he is. Very hard to keep up with. He's cost me a fortune but it's worth it. Left on my own, I couldn't decorate a closet. I have absolutely no imagination. But I admire a perfect work of art. Although it's something we've yet to achieve. Since I've known him, Michael and I have redecorated my apartment eighteen times. Including this one. Eighteen times. Top to bottom. We're only half way through this one and already I know we'll have to start again. So I hope you can understand the frustration. And if Michael insulted you, I — we apologize.

MAN:

Well, thank you for explaining the situation. Although, as situations go, I have to admit, I don't really get it. Why would you go to all the trouble?

JOAN:

It is a lot of trouble, of course, yes. There are times when I've felt like giving up. Michael gives me the inspiration to keep searching for that perfect constellation of form, texture, and colour. We look on it as a lifetime challenge.

MAN:

A lifetime is a lot of time.

JOAN:

There are a lot of choices. Probably too many.

69

MAN:

It sounds to me like you'll never be satisfied.

JOAN:

Yes. It does, doesn't it? But one day we'll find what we're looking for.

MAN:

And then what?

JOAN:

Oh. What an interesting question. Perhaps it's a little too interesting. *calling* Michael!

MICHAEL:

I won't be compromised!

JOAN:

Nobody's compromising anybody. *to MAN* He thinks you're putting in your two-cents worth about the apartment. People usually do. They think they know how to decorate because they think they know what they like. I used to be the same. But I'm trying not to have any opinions now. Sometimes it's difficult to be objective though, isn't it? But one has to be. Especially if you live in it. After all, on a purely subjective level, my apartment looks ridiculous. And I don't even have a decent, comfortable bed to sleep in. So you can understand why it's necessary for us to disassociate ourselves from our personal feelings. Personal feelings are so difficult anyway. Whereas style is absolute. Whether it's absolutely this, or absolutely that.

> *Another window opens, and PERCY leans out. He emits an audible sigh. Inside, behind him, a party is in full-swing.*

PERCY:

Dreary, isn't it?

MAN:

Sorry?

PERCY:

My God I feel like jumping. Right here and now. I'd rather splatter my guts all over the pavement than go back in there.

JOAN:

Oh, don't do that darling. You leave too much up to chance. If you want to convey the right message, you may want to slash your wrists over a simple, pale cotton print, for instance. It has a stronger impact. More clarity.

MAN:

You don't really want to jump, do you?

JOAN:

Of course he doesn't. People don't jump from buildings anymore.

MAN:

Why not?

JOAN:

The trend is much lighter. More whimsical.

MAN:

He's talking about suicide.

PERCY:

No I'm not. I'm talking about dying of boredom.

JOAN:

Well, if you'll excuse me . . .

> *She starts to go.*

PERCY:

I wonder if you could do me a favour.

JOAN:

Yes?

PERCY:

I wonder if you could call next door here in about five minutes, asking for me and sounding quite urgent. Say your name is Rhonda. I'll give you the number.

JOAN:

I'd love to oblige you, darling, but I no longer have a telephone. It didn't fit in with the decor.

> *JOAN leaves and closes her window. the MAN and PERCY are left alone.*

PERCY:

Everybody has a telephone. Nobody doesn't have a telephone. How on earth does she survive?

MAN:

It wouldn't be so bad.

PERCY:

I'd be lost. I wouldn't have a single friend. As it is now, I have nine hundred and forty.

MAN:

Friends?

PERCY:

Yes.

MAN:

You have that many friends?

PERCY:

Yes. Isn't it fabulous? People are always saying "I can't *count* the number of friends I have!" When what they actually mean is that they only have a handful. Maybe two, three hundred. But I can, and I've got nine hundred and forty.

MAN:

I didn't think it was possible to be intimate with that many people.

72

PERCY:

Who said anything about being intimate? I couldn't care less about most of them.

MAN:

Well, then they're not really your friends, are they?

PERCY:

Why not?

MAN:

The whole idea of friendship is that you like someone.

PERCY:

Why would I like them? They're awful. What an odd notion!

MAN:

You don't like any of them.

PERCY:

Like is a big word. If we're counting friends that I *like*, I've actually got more sweaters. I've got two hundred and sixty-eight sweaters, but actually sort of *like* three of them. Of the friends I have — uh . . . let's see . . . *He thinks.* No. I don't really like her, but I *love* her work. Uh . . . can I count you?

MAN:

What? As a friend?

PERCY:

No. As a friend I *like*. I already count you as a friend.

MAN:

But I'm not.

PERCY:

I beg your pardon.

MAN:

I'm not your friend.

PERCY:

Oh. Well, I guess I'll have to put you in the "don't like" column, then.

MAN:

Don't put me in *any* column.

PERCY:

What?

MAN:

I don't want to be in one of your columns.

PERCY:

Well, where would you suggest I put you.

MAN:

Don't put me anywhere. You don't own me. I'm not a sweater.

PERCY:

What are you taking about? Of course you're not a sweater. You're not even *wearing* a sweater.

JENNIFER pokes her head through the same window.

PERCY:

Jennifer. I want you to meet a friend of mine.

MAN:

I'm not his friend.

JENNIFER:

Well, any friend of Jack's is a friend of mine.

MAN:

I'm — not — his — friend!

PERCY:

That's all right. I'm not Jack.

JENNIFER:

You're not? Why aren't you?

PERCY:

Because I'm Percy.

JENNIFER:

Yes — well . . . It's the details that start to ruin a perfectly good relationship. I like to know as little about a person as possible. Preferably nothing at all.

Now AL leans out the same window.

AL:

I hope you guys don't think this is the way out.

PERCY:

Not unless you want to jump.

All laugh.

MAN:

What's so funny about that?

AL: *to MAN*

Hi! Don't I know you?

MAN:

No.

AL:

Are you sure?

MAN:

Of course I'm sure.

JENNIFER:

I don't know a soul.

PERCY:

Well, I can introduce you. They're all my friends.

75

AL:

Are they? Well, they're certainly not mine.

JENNIFER:

I don't even know which one is the host.

AL:

I am.

JENNIFER:

Oh! Well, it's a fabulous party. I wasn't invited. That's the only reason I'm here.

PERCY:

It's the best party I've been to in a long time. I've been to one hundred and eleven parties this year, and this is one of the best. Oh! Look! I think I see a friend of mine. Excuse me, will you?

PERCY leaves.

AL:

Who's *he*?

JENNIFER: *referring to MAN*

A friend of *his*.

AL:

Oh!

MAN:

No. He's not.

AL:

Well, whoever he is, I hope he leaves and takes everybody else with him. Except for you two, of course.

JENNIFER:

I'm afraid I can't stay. As much as I'm enjoying this one, I'm due at another party any minute now.

AL:

Oh? Who's party?

JENNIFER:

I'm sure you know her.

AL:

Probably.

JENNIFER:

But I can't remember her name. I'm not sure I even know her address. It's . . . somewhere.

AL:

I'd love to come.

JENNIFER:

Why don't you? Why don't you both come?

MAN:

I wasn't invited. I don't even know what you're talking about.

JENNIFER: *to AL, referring to MAN*

I just love your friend. He's so specific.

As she goes.

AL:

Isn't he!

She's gone.

AL:

Who's *she*?

MAN:

I haven't got any idea.

AL:

You meet the worst people at your own party.

MAN:
> Then why give a party?

AL:
> Well, I don't want to be antisocial. Don't get me wrong. I love parties. If only it wasn't for the people at them. But this is really the worst part, isn't it?

MAN:
> What is?

AL:
> The actual event. It's always such a crushing disappointment. From the minute the first guests arrive, I just want to evaporate into thin air. At my last party, I had to start a fire in the kitchen to get rid of them.

MAN:
> You started a fire!?

AL:
> Just a small one. But there was a lot of smoke. It cleared the place out quite nicely. It wasn't fifteen minutes before I was finally alone again.

MAN:
> Someone could have been seriously hurt.

AL:
> Oh, the fire department was there instantaneously. I called them ahead of time. But I'll never try that one again. There was a hell of a mess. This time I'm taking a more subtle approach. There's no food, no drinks, and the music is far too loud. Lots of people have already left.

> *Another window opens. NURSE WILSON pokes her head out.*

NURSE WILSON:
> Turn that God-awful music down!

AL:

I was actually planning on turning it up!

NURSE WILSON:

Oh, were you? Well, we'll just see about that!

AL:

Why don't you call the police, if you don't like it.

NURSE WILSON:

That's exactly what I intend to do!

AL:

If you do call, though — please don't tell them about all the drugs.

NURSE WILSON:

Drugs!

She goes inside.

AL:

Well, thank God for the neighbours. This thing might have gone on forever, and we've got that other party to go to. You don't happen to remember the address, do you?

MAN:

No.

AL:

Well, someone else is bound to know. That's where all these people will be going after they've been herded out of here.

MAN:

Why would you bother getting rid of them, just to follow them to another party?

AL:

I'm always hearing about parties I didn't go to. How great they were. What a fabulous time everybody had. The ones I miss are always the good ones. So I never miss one now. Are you coming?

MAN:

I don't like parties.

AL:

Why did you come to this one, then?

MAN:

I didn't.

AL:

Well, what are you doing here?

MAN:

Actually —

AL:

You're not thinking about jumping, are you? It's seven storeys.

MAN:

Yes. I know.

AL:

A guy could kill himself.

MAN:

Well . . . yes . . . he could, but . . .

The next window opens.

NURSE WILSON:

I called the police!

AL:

This guy's gonna jump, lady.

NURSE WILSON:

Really!

AL:

You sure you wouldn't rather go to this party?

NURSE WILSON:
>If he wants to jump, why don't you let him?

MAN:
>Look — I didn't say I wanted to. I don't know what I'm doing.
>I really —

NURSE WILSON:
>Would you like us to convince you?

LILLIAN: *a voice from inside*
>Is that Albert?

NURSE WILSON: *to LILLIAN*
>No. It isn't Albert. It's a man. He's thinking about jumping
>off the side of the building.

LILLIAN: *inside*
>Why doesn't he then?

NURSE WILSON: *to LILLIAN*
>That's what I asked him.

MAN:
>Look — this has nothing to do with either of *you*. Why don't
>you both go inside and just carry on with your lives?

AL:
>You don't mind if I go to this party then?

MAN:
>No. Of course I don't mind.

AL:
>It's not that I don't care about your plight or anything. It's just
>such a downer — that's all. Anyway, this lady looks pretty
>serious. Maybe she can talk you out of it.

NURSE WILSON:
>I am serious and I'm not talking him out of anything.

AL:
> Look — the police'll be here any minute. Just hang on until they get here. I gotta go. I don't even know where I'm going so who knows how long it'll take to get there.

> *AL goes, closing his window.*

NURSE WILSON:
> Some friend.

MAN:
> He's not a friend.

LILLIAN: *inside*
> Albert?

NURSE WILSON: *to LILLIAN*
> It's not Albert, Mrs. Wright. Albert's gone! He FLEW AWAY!!

LILLIAN:
> Why?

NURSE WILSON:
> You *know* why. Because he's a *bird*. *to MAN* God I hate old people.

LILLIAN: *inside*
> Who's a bird?

NURSE WILSON:
> Albert! Albert's a bird. We let him go, remember? We let him go because he was unhappy.

LILLIAN: *inside*
> Oh!

NURSE WILSON:
> She remembers the whole thing.

LILLIAN: *inside*
> No I don't!

NURSE WILSON:
> She's supposed to be deaf but she can hear the grass growing. So what's stopping you?

MAN:
> Huh?

NURSE WILSON:
> What's stopping you from jumping? Wait — let me guess. You're afraid of heights. Now that's a pity. Letting a little thing like that stand in the way of your suicide, when really it's such a perfectly logical thing to do.

MAN:
> Logical?

NURSE WILSON:
> I started out my career thinking I wanted to save people's lives. Imagine!

MAN:
> I think that's very noble.

NURSE WILSON:
> A lot you know. Where's the nobility in watching people hang on to the last shred of a meagre existence? Hooked up to every imaginable medical apparatus. Jumping is the only way to go these days, otherwise you run the serious risk of a protracted survival. My! Doesn't the sidewalk look inviting from here!

MAN:
> I'd rather not look down if you don't mind.

NURSE WILSON:
> Aren't you even the least bit curious?

MAN:
> I can imagine what it's like.

NURSE WILSON:
> I suppose you expect me to ask you what your reasons are for jumping.

MAN:
You're probably not interested.

NURSE WILSON:
You're probably right.

MAN:
Nobody seems terribly interested.

NURSE WILSON:
Why should they be? Death isn't terribly interesting. I work in a hospital when I'm not here cleaning up after this thing and I can tell you first hand, death isn't the least bit interesting. In fact — it's very routine. Besides people are too busy to be interested in other people's problems. These days you have to pay someone to be interested.

MAN:
Busy doing what?

NURSE WILSON:
Finding reasons not to jump themselves.

MAN:
So what's your reason?

NURSE WILSON:
Me? I'm a humanitarian.

MAN:
You don't seem the type.

NURSE WILSON:
Oh? What type is that?

MAN:
You don't seem very — well — very friendly.

NURSE WILSON:
Why should I be friendly. I despise almost everyone I meet.

MAN:
I thought humanitarians were supposed to *like* people.

NURSE WILSON:
I like people on the whole. It's individuals I can't stand.

LILLIAN: *from inside*
Has he jumped yet?

NURSE WILSON:
No. He's vacillating.

LILLIAN: *inside*
What?

NURSE WILSON:
He hasn't made up his mind, yet — one way or the other.

LILLIAN:
He shouldn't be so tentative.

MAN:
I *have* made up my mind.

NURSE WILSON:
Oh. *to LILLIAN* He has made up his mind. The
police will be here soon. You'd better go now or they'll definitely
talk you out of it. They're experts. They listen to all your
problems. They sympathize with every one of them. Eventually,
they convince you that life has some meaning. That there's some
little thread to hang onto. So you hang on, as they slowly reel
you in. But you never let go again, not for the rest of your life.
The next thing you know, you're old, and by that time you've
been hanging on so long and so tightly to that little thread that
it practically has to be pried loose.

MAN:
You know something — you're astonishingly morbid.

LILLIAN: *close to the window.*
What seems to be the problem?

85

NURSE WILSON:
I already told you, Mrs. Wright. I'm not going to tell you again.

LILLIAN: *appearing now in window*
Well, get out of my way then.

NURSE WILSON:
You're not supposed to be up and around.

LILLIAN:
Where is this man?

NURSE WILSON:
Die of heart failure. See if I care.

LILLIAN:
She doesn't really want me to die because then she'd have to fill out a form.

NURSE WILSON:
I've already filled it out!

LILLIAN:
I'm a hundred years old. Does that impress you?

MAN:
That's very old.

LILLIAN:
Yes. They send people like her to look after me.

MAN:
She's not very nice.

LILLIAN:
She doesn't have a very nice job. Looking after sick people. Waiting for them to die. So she thinks that she has to pretend she has no feelings.

NURSE WILSON:
I haven't!

LILLIAN:

But she's afraid.   *NURSE WILSON goes.*   Don't pay
any attention to her.

Pause.

LILLIAN:

Oh my, what a lovely evening.

MAN:

I never noticed.

LILLIAN:

I haven't looked out this window in years. I used to go out on
evenings like this. I walked down to the end of that street and
took the streetcar as far as it went. Up where there weren't any
houses. That's where we stopped. That's where the streetcar
turned around. As though the world was flat, and that was the
end of it, where you fell off. That was about seventy years ago,
so I imagine the houses go quite a bit further now. But not far
enough, of course. I imagine the streetcar eventually stops
somewhere and turns around.

MAN:

There isn't any streetcar.

LILLIAN.

There isn't?

MAN:

There hasn't been one for about thirty years.

LILLIAN:

Well, that just goes to show you what I know. I haven't gone
out since . . . well, in about fifty years.

MAN:

Fifty years?

LILLIAN:

Well, as I said — you can really only go out so far, and then you've got to turn around and come back. I find that somewhat limiting. I prefer to go nowhere at all. As it turns out my apartment is much larger than I thought. In fact, it's enormous.

MAN:

It can't be more than a few hundred square feet at the most.

LILLIAN:

Yes. It's almost too much to grasp, isn't it? Of course, it looks a lot smaller now. Since she came to look after me. She cleaned it all up. Put everything in order. Kicked Albert out. She has a very sanitary point of view. Doesn't like pigeons. I imagine he'll come back though. When he's had enough of flying.

NURSE WILSON: *inside*

He's not coming back in here.

LILLIAN:

I used to have all kinds of things piled up against this window. Until *they* came and took everything away. And once Albert saw the window, there was just no keeping him. After all those years, his little head was suddenly filled with big ideas.

MAN:

All what years?

LILLIAN:

Those years.

MAN:

Pigeons don't live that long.

LILLIAN:

How long?

MAN:

How many years are we talking about exactly?

LILLIAN:

Oh, I don't know. About fifty.

MAN:

That doesn't make any sense.

LILLIAN:

No. It doesn't.

Pause

LILLIAN:

Must be a riddle.

Pause

MAN:

I don't get it.

LILLIAN:

Neither do I. Well — it's just a story. It's not important. People attach too much importance to these things. That reminds me of another story.

MAN waits as she loses her train of thought. Finally, he coughs, which arouses her.

LILLIAN:

Oh, my! What a lovely evening.

MAN:

You were going to tell me something?

LILLIAN:

What about?

MAN:

I don't know. Something reminded you of a story.

LILLIAN:

A story? — Let's see . . .

A long pause.

MAN:

I guess you don't remember. It's not important. Really. I
thought — I thought it might be — well — important, somehow.

LILLIAN:

You're looking for something important.

MAN:

No. Well, I — I need — I'm looking for something, yes.

LILLIAN:

I don't have anything. Just an empty room. It'll be coming up
for rent soon, if you're interested.

MAN:

No. I'm not looking for a room.

LILLIAN:

It's a place to hang your hat. To sort out all your shoes.

MAN:

I don't need to sort out my shoes. All my shoes are the same.
Every pair identical. All seven pairs. I have seven hats also. All
like this one. I have one for every day of the week. Only I can't
remember what day it is.

LILLIAN:

Oh.

MAN:

I've lost track, you see. I went to sleep and I had a dream. I
— I think it was a dream. I dreamt that I got up, and made
my way to work, and when work was over I came home and
went to bed. And then I woke up. I think I woke up.

LILLIAN:

It's Wednesday.

MAN:

It is?

90

LILLIAN:

I don't know, but I thought it would make you feel better.

MAN: *now he speaks slowly and deliberately, in an attempt to understand his own words*

Not really. You see — my faith in the days of the week has been seriously undermined. When I woke up this morning, I wasn't exactly sure what day it was. And for that brief moment — it was only a matter of seconds — I think it was seconds — I stood — or I should say I "lay" on very shaky ground. After all — how could I act with assuredness. How could I rise up and plunge headlong into Friday's world, if it was actually Saturday? And so I lay completely still for a moment, pondering this question. That's when I noticed my hands. I'd never noticed them before. How they moved with amazing dexterity. But this flexibility, this movement of hands, can never extend beyond the boundaries of it's own flesh — can only reach as far as the fingertips and no further, much as the movement of time is restricted by the days of the week. So I got up and tried to erase these things from my mind. I tried to get dressed. But then I began to understand other things — for example the meaning of shoes. They were little prisons for my feet. Absolute definitions of space. I could run a million miles, in any direction, and still not escape them. And my hat — forming a firm idea around my head, as if to say, Well, that's about the size of it. My mind could expand into infinite space, and still never change the shape of my head. I saw in the mirror a condemned man, serving a life sentence inside his body. Even the car — I drove — to work. My car. This thing. This instrument of liberation. It wasn't freedom. It was merely the idea of freedom, bound in metal. A kind of hope, but with a speed limit attached to it. Now I was travelling an unknown route along a familiar road. It led in exactly the direction I was going, but not by coincidence. The asphalt was not laying itself a path in front of me. I was merely following a prearranged course and then something happened, something that had never happened before. When I finally arrived in town at my usual space it was taken. I was late for work you see and there was another car in my space. Someone had taken my space you see. I sat in my car for a moment, not knowing where to go. Just staring straight ahead. And then, I put my car into gear and drove into it. Drove right into this other car. There didn't seem to be any other choice. No place else to go, you see.

So I put my car in reverse, backed up, and rammed into this car again. And then again, and again and again, until finally this other car, this intruder of my space was smashed up against the side of the building, like an accordion. So now I had my space back, and I parked. I got out of the car, and turned to head for my office. That's when I realized. It wasn't my space at all. Somehow I got completely turned around. This wasn't anywhere near where I work. I didn't know where I was. I hadn't any idea. I had always depended on the road which lead there. The way I've always believed that one thing leads to another. Then I saw this building. I thought I'd come up here to get a better perspective on my exact situation. And from here the view is quite clear. There are no spaces left, you see. I have no place to park my car.

LILLIAN:
Have you tried The Bay?

MAN:
Don't you understand?

LILLIAN:
Of course I understand. You didn't need to make such a long speech. When you're a hundred years old you'll understand everything. And then you'll die.

MAN:
Why wait?

LILLIAN:
Something interesting might happen. But then again, it might not. I think you should jump now.

MAN:
You do?

LILLIAN:
If that's what you want to do, I think you should do it.

MAN:
There really is no reason to live, is there?

LILLIAN:
Not really.

MAN: *as he prepares to jump*
It's sort of disappointing. I wonder where they'll tow my car.

LILLIAN:
Oh. Now I remember!

MAN: *stopping*
What?

LILLIAN:
That story. Some years ago, I went to Paris to see the *Mona Lisa*.
It's in the Louvre, the largest building in the world, probably.
But the *Mona Lisa*, as it turns out, is very small. So naturally
I couldn't find it. I kept looking for something — big. Then I
saw a huge crowd of people all standing around — looking
disappointed. And there she was — smiling as if she knew.

MAN:
That's it? That's the whole story?

LILLIAN:
You do like a long story, don't you. Let's see. There was a young
Frenchman standing next to me, in a terrible state of despair.
He began talking to me as if he'd known me all his life. I didn't
understand a word he was saying, but he didn't seem to take
any notice. I thought I'd lose him in the crowd, but he followed
me right out of the museum. He told me a very long and involved
story, often punctuating the words with his fists. Occasionally
he would sink into a sadness the like of which I'd never seen.
And then he would start raving again. The further we walked,
the more distressed he became — the more enraged. By the time
we reached the Pont Neuf he was sobbing uncontrollably. It
seemed very clear that he wanted me to say something. We
hadn't walked halfway across, when he started to climb over the
side of the bridge. I didn't know what to say. So I blurted out

93

the only thing in French that I'd ever learned. *"La pamplemousse est sur la table."* I don't even know what it means. But he responded very positively. He thought about it for a moment, and then smiled. After that his mood changed considerably. In fact, he was delighted. Whatever it was I said, it seemed to be something for him to hang his hat on. And he walked away a new man. Determined, it seemed, to live by this philosophy the rest of his life.

MAN:
It doesn't mean anything

LILLIAN:
It must mean something. I learned it in school.

MAN:
"The grapefruit is on the table"?

LILLIAN:
Oh. Is that what it means?   *pause*   Well, that's not a bad philosophy to live by. As philosophies go. It has a certain — preciseness.

MAN:
How have you managed to stay alive so long?

LILLIAN:
I forget.

MAN:
Shut up in your room like that? Never going out?

LILLIAN:
There are other places to go besides *out*. There's *in*. There's *around*. There's *under*. *Over*. *Between*.

MAN:
Down.

LILLIAN:
Well, you might go down. But you might go up. If you're going

94

to go to all the trouble of jumping, you might as well try going up and see what happens. Albert went up. Straight up.

MAN:
Albert was a pigeon.

LILLIAN:
He didn't know that. Not for sure. He'd never flown a day in his whole life, not until the day we let him go. You could be the first of a kind. Imagine what a story that would make! You'd be interviewed by just about every newspaper in the world. You'd travel around giving lectures. You'd be an inspiration to others. There'd be people flying all over the place. That sort of thing has to start somewhere. It might as well start with you. If you're going to give your life up anyway, you may as well give it up to something. The principle is very simple. You just have to let go and let the wind currents do the rest. You know about airflow, don't you?

MAN:
I really don't think . . .

LILLIAN:
No. Don't think. The important thing is to just let it happen. Let it take you where it wants. Don't try to go any place special this first time. Just do a circle once around the building, and come back. Once you get a better feel for it, you can go a little further.

Suddenly, a huge spotlight on MAN.

POLICE MEGAPHONE:
Stop! This is the police!

LILLIAN:
Go!

MAN:
I don't know what to do — I can't — fly —

POLICE MEGAPHONE:
Just stay calm. Don't move.

LILLIAN:
Don't listen to them. They're all trying to put the world in order.
They don't want people flying around all over the place. They'd
have to make up a whole bunch of new regulations. That's just
bullshit. Just go.

MAN:
Are you sure?

LILLIAN:
Just up and away.

POLICE MEGAPHONE:
Stop!

MAN:
Just like that?

POLICE MEGAPHONE:
Stay right where you are!

MAN:
I'm supposed to stay right where I am.

LILLIAN:
Go!

MAN:
All right — I'm going.

LILLIAN:
Then go!

MAN:
Goodbye!

A blackout.

Ahhhhhhhhhhhhhhhhhhhhhhhhhh!

As the lights come up the MAN flies with the aid of his umbrella. He then lands on the ledge of another building. Four people open their windows.

ONE:
We saw that.

MAN:
What?

TWO:
We saw you fly over here from that building across the street.

MAN:
You did?

THREE:
We've been watching the whole thing.

MAN:
You have?

FOUR:
Yes. We have.

TWO:
We saw you talk to that old lady.

FOUR:
To all those people.

TWO:
We saw the whole thing from beginning to end.

THREE:
And then we saw you fly over here and land!

FOUR:
There's just one thing . . .

TWO:
> We don't get it.

ONE:
> What's the flying supposed to represent? Is it an existential statement or what?

TWO:
> It's a Jungian thing, isn't it?

THREE:
> I don't agree. I think it's political.

ONE:
> Is it about enlightenment?

THREE:
> There's a suggestion of mass revolt.

TWO:
> There's an archetypal quality about it.

ONE:
> I detect strong religious overtones.

THREE:
> It's a struggle against tyranny, isn't it?

FOUR:
> I think it's just weird.

MAN:
> Will you excuse me?

> *Suddenly the MAN is airborne and he flies through the stars. He then returns to the original window ledge. LILLIAN is gone. Below, an ambulance light flashes. The MAN knocks at the window.*

MAN:
> Hello! HELLO - O!!

NURSE WILSON appears.

NURSE WILSON:
Yes?

MAN:
The old lady. I'd like to speak to her. I have to tell·her about
— something — something quite incredible!!

NURSE WILSON:
Yeah . . . well, she's gone.

MAN:
Gone?

They look down.

MAN:
So sudden? She was here just a few minutes ago.

NURSE WILSON:
Yeah, well . . . that's the way it always happens. So — what's
this "something incredible"? As if I really want to know.

MAN:
It was . . . it was nothing.

NURSE WILSON:
I thought you were going to jump off the ledge.

MAN:
I did.

NURSE WILSON:
Oh. You did, did you?

MAN:
Yes, I did. I flew across the street to that building and back.

NURSE WILSON:
I suppose you want to come inside now.

MAN:

    I'm just fine where I am.

NURSE WILSON:

    You can't stay perched out there forever.

MAN:

    Why not?

NURSE WILSON:

    Because it's abnormal behaviour.

MAN:

    Not for a pigeon.

NURSE WILSON:

    You're not a PIGEON!!

MAN:

    Yes . . . I know that now.

    She goes.

MAN:

    But for a moment . . . for a brief . . . moment . . . I didn't know. And the wind carried me up and took me along for a ride. And I forgot. I forgot my own story . . . and I flew . . . flew on the wings of someone else's.

POLICE MEGAPHONE:

    This is the police.

MAN:

    I have to forget . . . try . . . to forget everything. Forget everything that has ever happened to me . . . everything that ever *will* happen . . . everything . . . and wait . . . just wait for the wind again . . . and do nothing . . . nothing . . . and . . . wait . . . just . . . . .

    The sound of the wind increases and the music, as the lights fade. In the blackout we hear the police megaphone.

POLICE MEGAPHONE:

All right, ladies and gentlemen — break it up. Just break it up now and go home. Come on, move along — move along now ladies and gentlemen. Everything will be fine. Everything's under control, so let's just disperse with this little gathering and go home. The show's over.

The End.

Definision

Connect with other

quiet
louder !

animal claw